THE MONKEY AND THE BEE

BY C. P. BLOOM
ILLUSTRATED BY PETER RAYMUNDO

ABRAMS BOOKS FOR YOUNG READERS
NEW YORK

Dedicated to Dan Lazar
and Tamar Brazis,
who helped bring
our monkey to life.
—C. P. Bloom

Library of Congress Cataloging-in-Publication Data
Bloom, C. P.
  The monkey and the bee / by C.P. Bloom ;
illustrated by Peter Raymundo.
    pages cm
  ISBN 978-1-4197-0886-2
[1. Bees–Fiction. 2. Monkeys–Fiction. 3. Friendship–
Fiction. 4. Humorous stories.] I. Raymundo, Peter,
illustrator. II. Title.
  PZ7.B62277Mo 2015
  [E]–dc23
  2014015636

Text copyright © 2015 C. P. Bloom
Illustrations copyright © 2015 Peter Raymundo
Book design by Chad W. Beckerman
  and Pamela Notarantonio
Published in 2015 by Abrams Books for Young
Readers, an imprint of ABRAMS. All rights
reserved. No portion of this book may be
reproduced, stored in a retrieval system, or
transmitted in any form or by any means,
mechanical, electronic, photocopying, recording,
or otherwise, without written permission from
the publisher.

Printed and bound in China
10 9 8 7 6 5 4 3 2 1

ABRAMS
THE ART OF BOOKS SINCE 1949
115 West 18th Street
New York, NY 10011
www.abramsbooks.com

THE
BEE

THE
BaNaNa

FLICK!

THE BEE

THE BEE!

THE
BEE

THE
BEE

THE
MONKEY

THE LION

THE MONKEY AND THE BEE